What Grew in Larry's Garden

For Miriam, Maggie and Iain — L.A.

To everyone who takes the time
to make their community a more
vibrant place — K.R.

Text © 2020 Laura Alary
Illustrations © 2020 Kass Reich

Acknowledgment
With thanks to Larry Zacharko for the inspiration. — L.A.

Kids Can Press gratefully acknowledges the financial support of the Government
of Ontario, through Ontario Creates; the Ontario Arts Council; the Canada
Council for the Arts; and the Government of Canada for our publishing activity.

Published in Canada and the U.S. by Kids Can Press Ltd.
25 Dockside Drive, Toronto, ON M5A 0B5

Kids Can Press is a Corus Entertainment Inc. company

www.kidscanpress.com

The artwork in this book was rendered with gouache paint
and colored pencils, with final touches added digitally.

The text is set in Minya Nouvelle.

Edited by Jennifer Stokes
Designed by Julia Naimska

Printed and bound in Shenzhen, China, in 10/2019 by C & C Offset

CM 20 0 9 8 7 6 5 4 3 2 1

Library and Archives Canada Cataloguing in Publication

Title: What grew in Larry's garden / written by Laura Alary ; illustrated by
Kass Reich.

Names: Alary, Laura, author. | Reich, Kass, illustrator.

Identifiers: Canadiana 20190085177 | ISBN 9781525301087 (hardcover)

Classification: LCC PS8601.L264 W53 2020 | DDC jC813/.6 — dc23

What Grew in Larry's Garden

Laura Alary   Kass Reich

KIDS CAN PRESS

In a sprawling city,
 in a leafy neighborhood,
  on a narrow street,
   in a cozy house
    with a tiny yard
     lived a girl named Grace.

Next door, in a yard just as tiny, Grace's neighbor Larry had a garden.

In his garden, Larry grew all sorts of vegetables. But not ordinary ones. There were buttery yellow carrots and purple potatoes. Rainbow chard and scarlet runner beans. Rosy tomatoes the color of ripe peaches. And black ones with red insides.

"You won't find these in most grocery stores,"
declared Larry, admiring a zebra-striped tomato.
Grace thought Larry's garden was one of the
wonders of the world.

Every spare moment she had, Grace helped Larry in his garden. Together they watered and weeded.

Planted and pruned.

Hoed and harvested.

And when bugs burrowed into the carrots, and slugs and snails chewed the lettuce, Grace and Larry solved the problem together.

"We can figure this out," said Larry.

At the library, Grace learned that lots of bugs don't like the smell of marigolds. Grace and Larry planted marigolds among the carrots, and the bugs disappeared.

As for the slugs and snails, they picked them off with their bare fingers.

"Our hard work will be worth it," said Larry, popping a slug into a bucket. "This is important. We're not just growing vegetables!"

"What are we growing?" asked Grace.

"Wait and see," said Larry.

Keeping squirrels away from the tomatoes was a bigger problem.

"We can figure this out," said Larry, scratching his head.

They built little cages out of wire. The tomato plants could grow inside the wire, but the squirrels could not get at the fruit.

"Sometimes fences are handy," said Larry.

When summer ended and autumn came, Grace helped Larry gather and dry seeds to save for next spring. Later that winter, they started growing the tomato seeds in little cups. There were hundreds of them.

Larry, a teacher, took the tomato seedlings to school so his students could look after them.

"What will they do with all these plants?" Grace wanted to know.

"That's the best part," replied Larry. "These are not just tomato plants."

"What are they?" asked Grace.

"Wait and see," said Larry.

Winter melted away and spring sprouted. One warm afternoon, Grace found Larry on his porch with a pile of papers in his lap.

"You wanted to know what my students would do with our plants," he said. "Listen to these letters."

Dear Friend,

I'm the kid who used to steal pears from your trees. I am giving you this tomato plant to say sorry.

Sincerely,
Matthew

Dear Bus Driver,

I rode on your school bus for years. You were always so friendly to all the kids. I am giving you this tomato plant to say thank you.

From,
Adira

Dear Mrs. Bianchi,

I live next door to you, but we hardly ever talk. You have the most amazing flower garden. It makes me happy just to see it. I am giving you this tomato plant to tell you that you make the world more beautiful for a lot of people.

Best wishes,
Amrit

"My students will give the plants away, and they wrote these letters to tell why," explained Larry. "Every plant is a gift, a little green tendril reaching out to someone. Connecting people."

"Now I see!" cried Grace. "We were growing a whole lot more than tomatoes!"

"Exactly!" said Larry.

But a shadow fell.

One afternoon, Grace went outside and found Larry sitting among his tomatoes. The plants looked wilted. So did Larry. And then Grace saw why. The neighbor on the other side had added a big panel to the top of his fence, blocking out the sun on Larry's garden.

"So much for my tomatoes," Larry said sadly.

The looming fence made the garden seem smaller than ever. Just a tiny patch of earth. Grace looked at the drooping tomato plants and thought about how they spread kindness.

She gave Larry a hug. "We can figure this out," she said.

Larry went next door to speak to his neighbor. But they could not agree.

"He says the fence makes him feel safe," said Larry with a sigh.

"I guess that makes sense," said Grace slowly, thinking about the handy fence that protected the tomato plants from hungry squirrels. "But ... I have another idea."

"What's that?" wondered Larry.

"Wait and see," replied Grace.

The next morning, when Larry's neighbor stepped outside to get the newspaper, there on the porch was a small pot, a packet of seeds and a note.

Dear Neighbor,

I live two doors down from you, and I like to help Larry in his garden. I am giving you these seeds to say I hope we can all be friends. I think having good friends is the best way to feel safe.

Sincerely,
Grace

P.S. I have a plan. Could you meet me outside on Saturday morning?

That weekend, Larry heard hammering. When he went outside, he found Grace in the yard next door, working side by side with his neighbor. The high panel on the fence was gone. So was the shadow. Now they were pounding nails into the fence and tying strings to make a kind of ladder.

"Larry!" cried Grace. "Come and see!"

Larry peered over the fence and saw seed packets.

"We're planting beans," explained Grace. "They're going to climb the fence!"

Larry's neighbor looked up from the string he was knotting. "I figured we could put this fence to better use," he said.

That afternoon, Larry and Grace and their
neighbor sat down together and feasted on fresh
lemonade and cherry tomatoes from Larry's garden.
They were still warm from the sun.

Author's Note

"To see things in the seed, that is genius." — Lao Tzu

If seeing things in seeds is a form of genius, then Larry Zacharko has a rare gift.

Few people would see much possibility in a tiny urban backyard and a handful of tomato seeds. But Larry has spent his life in gardens, soaking in their mysteries and miracles. He knows that something that appears as dry and dead as a seed can suddenly burst into life and color.

Larry Zacharko, whose story inspired this book, is a real person, and his tomato project is something he really does with his students. When he started teaching, Larry was faced with a classroom full of students who had troubles both at home and at school. He saw possibility in them, too. Working with what he had — soil, seeds and a greenhouse no one was using — Larry showed his students how to get their hands dirty. Kids who could not sit still in class found focus and calm when they worked with plants. And Larry began to see a new possibility — a project that would take his students beyond the greenhouse and into the community.

Larry encouraged each student to personally deliver an heirloom tomato plant — started from seed during class — to someone in their neighborhood. And they were to include a letter with the plant, explaining why that neighbor had been chosen to receive the gift.

The students were terrified. Growing tomatoes was one thing; knocking on the doors of people they hardly knew was a different matter. They worried that people wouldn't trust them. Larry, however, was sure that if they could get past the fear, amazing things might happen.

He was not disappointed.

One student gave a plant to a woman in his apartment building whose son had died. "I wanted to let her know that there's still life in the world," he explained. Another described how he fearfully thrust a plant and letter into the hands of the grumpy old man down the street, then ran away. A few months later, the man surprised him with a gift: a brown paper bag full of heirloom tomatoes.

One encounter at a time, the students were growing community.

Growing anything takes patience. If you give plants what they need — water, sunshine, gentleness, room to grow — they will thrive. Possibility hides in every seed. Each year, Larry's students continue to find possibility in seeds, and in themselves, growing their community one plant at a time.